Cinderella

A Folk and Fairy Tales Reader

For Flora Ng

by **Liza Charlesworth**
illustrated by **Ian Smith**

Text copyright © 2016 by Liza Charlesworth
Illustrations copyright © 2016 Scholastic Inc.

ISBN: 978-1-338-09427-5

10 9 8 7 6 5 4 3 2 1   16 17 18 19 20

Printed in the U.S.A.   40
First printing 2016

Book design by Maria Mercado

SCHOLASTIC INC.

W9-CEA-741

Cinderella was so sad.

She could not go to the ball.

Poof!
She met a fairy.

Poof!
She got a new dress.

Poof!
She got new shoes.

Poof!
She got a new car.

She went to the ball.

She danced with the prince.

Oh, no!
She had to go.

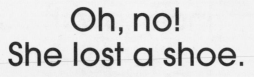

Oh, no!
She lost a shoe.

The prince saw the shoe.

The prince saw the girl.

The shoe fit!

Cinderella was so happy.

Comprehension Boosters

1. What three magic things did the fairy make for Cinderella?

Shoes, Adress and a car.

2. Why was Cinderella so happy at the end of the story? *Because she ma the princ got a b life.*

3. Would you like to be a prince or princess? Tell why or why not. *I would rather be a princess because I am a girl.*